SLEEPY SHEEPY

by LUCY RUTH CUMMINS

Illustrated by PETE OSWALD

Flamingo Books

FLAMINGO BOOKS

An imprint of Penguin Random House LLC, New York

First published in the United States of America by Flamingo Books, an imprint of Penguin Random House LLC, 2023

Text copyright © 2023 by Lucy Ruth Cummins
Illustrations copyright © 2023 by Pete Oswald

Visit us online at penguinrandomhouse.com.

Library of Congress Cataloging-in-Publication Data is available.

Manufactured in Italy

ISBN 9780593465912

1   3   5   7   9   10   8   6   4   2

LEG

Design by Pete Oswald and Jim Hoover   Text set in Kabouter

For Jakey —L. R. C.
For Blake —P. O.

Sleepy Sheepy . . .

WAS NOT

SLEEPY!

But it was time for bed.

(At least that's what the clock said.)

WAS

NOT

SLEEPY!

But
Sleepy Sheepy—
now *quite weepy*—

WAS NOT

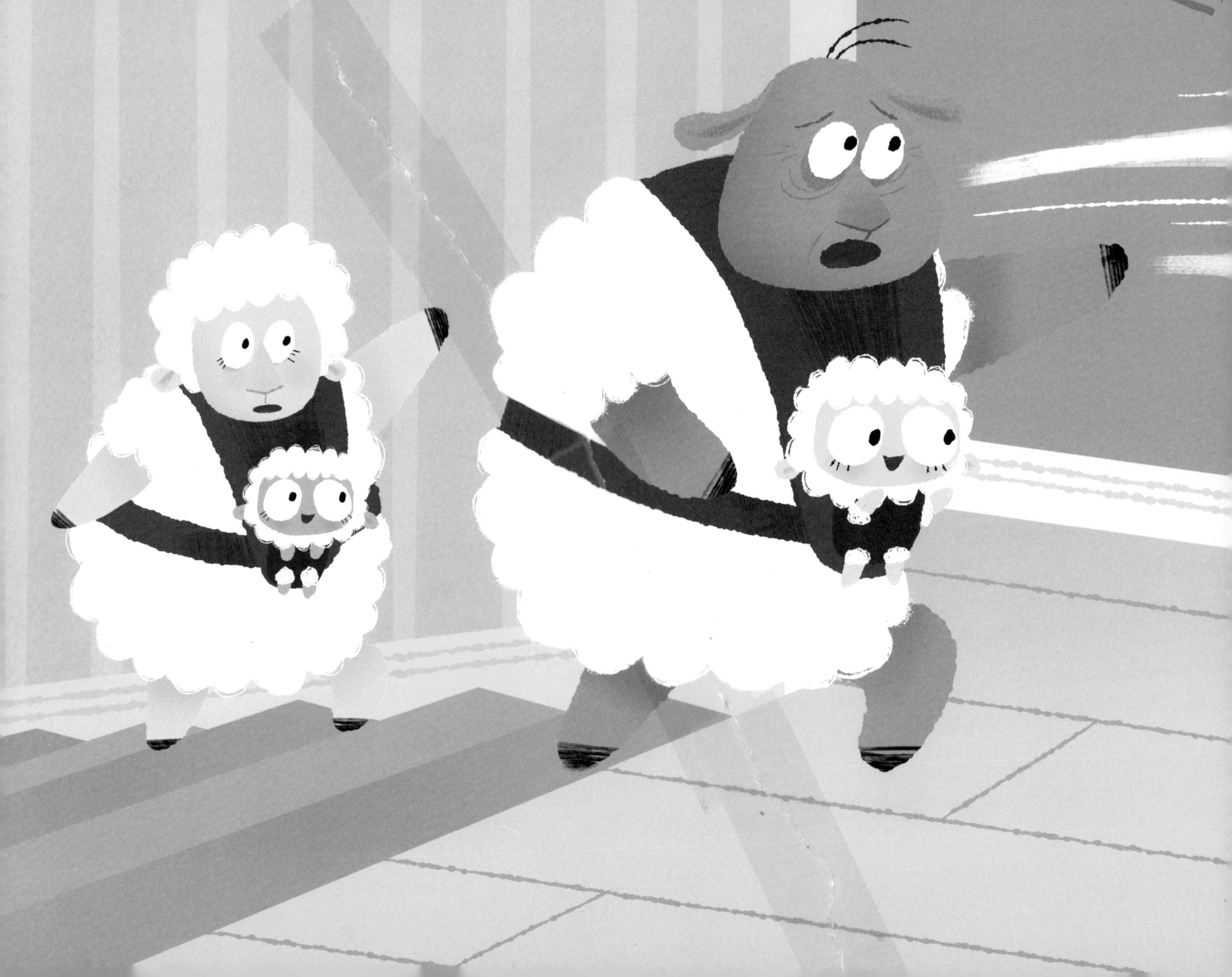

SLEEPY!

In fact,
Sleepy Sheepy
was . . .

WIDE—

Sleepy Sheepy WOULD NOT SLEEPY.

He was WIRED and absolutely NOT TIRED!

So instead of bed, he:

built with blocks,

knitted socks,

and spun Ma and Pa
Sheepy quite a yarn.

And just then, Sleepy Sheepy . . .

"See?" said Ma Sheepy.
"There!" said Pa Sheepy.

So then they trotted softly
hoof-in-hoof-in-hoof
to his snuggly-wuggly big boy bed.
But Sleepy Sheepy . . .

It was time for
a nighttime snack.
But!

His eyelids drooped.

His shoulders stooped.

His brain was pooped.

"Maybe ..." said Sleepy Sheepy
(quite sheepishly!),

"I'm a *little bit* tired."

So Sleepy Sheepy got
under the cozy covers.

Ma Sheepy gave Sleepy Sheepy
a kiss on his fluffy forehead.

Pa Sheepy tucked his covers in
quite tight (which felt just right!).

And by the time they turned out the light...

Sleepy Sheepy
was fast a-sleepy.